CAPP STREET CARNIVAL

CAPP STREET CARNIVAL

SANDRA DUTTON

FARRAR STRAUS GIROUX
NEW YORK

Copyright © 2003 by Sandra Dutton
All rights reserved
Distributed in Canada by Douglas & McIntyre Ltd.
Printed in the United States of America
Designed by Barbara Grzeslo
First edition, 2003
1 3 5 7 9 10 8 6 4 2

Library of Congress Cataloging-in-Publication Data
Dutton, Sandra.
  Capp Street carnival / Sandra Dutton.
    p. cm.
  Summary: Eleven-year-old Mary Mae finds herself extremely busy
with her preparations for a fund-raising carnival and her friend
Annabelle's wedding, which are going to be one week apart.
  ISBN 0-374-31065-3
  [1. Carnivals—Fiction. 2. Weddings—Fiction.] I. Title.

PZ7.D952 Cap 2003
[Fic]—dc21

                                              2002021604

WITH LOVE FOR WAYNE,
WHO KNOWS THE TERRITORY

~

CONTENTS

CAPP STREET CARNIVAL

STUNTS

Me, I had on a big blue hat with fur trim. Truman Earlywine, he had on a business vest that barely stretched around his belly. And Virgil Hertz, he was in a coat with tails.

We was down at Lukey Chassoldt's doing stunts—walking along the porch rail, pretending to fall, stomping around, singing. I had me my guitar. Little Lukey—he was only two—he'd laugh and wave and spit, but just when we was getting warmed up, Mrs. Chassoldt said she had to take him inside, didn't want him getting too excited. She knowed we was trying to make him happy, but Lukey had a heart murmur. Means you're born with a hole in your heart.

So we come on down Capp Street to my house to figure out what to do next. Truman, he was shuffling some sandpaper blocks, and Hertz, he was plunking on some cans and cowbells he'd nailed to a piece of wood. It was dusk, best time to put on a show, and still warm out even though it was October. Then up the street come this four-door Plymouth, parks right in front of my house, and the driver, he don't get out of the car.

"Who's that?" Hertz asked.

"I bet that's Leroy Cuzzens," I said. "He's a-calling for Annabelle." Annabelle Gosset was our boarder. She lived upstairs in the spare bedroom and ate dinner with us every evening. Back in August, she'd moved up from Somerset, Kentucky, and took a job in the billing department at the Rise'n'Shine Poultry Company. Told us earlier that week she'd just been asked out by the assistant manager.

"Why don't he get out of the car?" asked Truman.

Leroy just set there working on a crossword puzzle, marking away with a big yellow pencil.

"Well, it ain't time yet," I said.

Annabelle had told Mama, Daddy, and me that

if Leroy Cuzzens arrived early, he'd set out in the car until the appointed hour. That's what she'd heard, anyway, from this girl at work.

Mama'd been real impressed. "Executives is always punctual," she'd said.

So here he was at 7:20, all duded up in a brown suit, collar so tight his neck looked like crescent rolls.

Hertz walked over and waved his arms to see if Leroy'd look up, but he didn't. He just kept working his crossword. Next thing we was all three walking around Leroy's car, just a-walking and a-walking around, not touching nothing, not doing nothing wrong. We was just sizing things up, seeing if he'd notice us.

We stopped up front, me in the middle, and all started singing one of our favorite tunes, "Will Your Daddy's Heart Be Broken If There's Parsnips in the Stew?" Me, I double-strummed my guitar, Truman slapped his sandpaper blocks, and Hertz plunked away on his cans.

But Leroy, he pretended he didn't see us, just kept working his crossword, glancing out the side window, like as if he was wallowing deep in his ABC's.

"I guess he don't like country," Truman said.

"Maybe he likes Mozart," Hertz said, and he put his board up on his shoulder like a violin and made like he was strumming it with a bow.

We started to dance the minuet, but that Leroy, he just touched his pencil to his tongue and stared up at the trees.

Hertz done a turn and a bow and we all three done a turn and a bow, only Hertz and Truman, they conked heads. Truman flopped down onto the ground howling, he thought everything was so funny.

Leroy rolled down the window, leaned out, and said to me, "Is your mother aware that you're out here?"

"Yes, my mother is a-*ware*," I said. And then I made up a song. I started strumming real fast and went,

AWARE, STARE, PARTRIDGE, PEAR

CAT'S IN THE OVEN AND DOG'S ON THE STAIR

OH WHERE OH WHERE OH WHERE OH WHERE

PARTRIDGE, PARTRIDGE, PARTRIDGE PEAR

I got louder and louder, and Hertz and Truman, they was coming in with their instruments. And then we all done another bow.

Leroy pushed his glasses up with his middle finger and leaned out the car window. "Well, if you don't mind, I'd like to finish this crossword in peace." He rolled his window back up.

So we left him alone, but when he went into the house, I followed him inside. Took my guitar off and done the same walk he done, chest out like a pigeon. Hertz and Truman went on over to Truman's house.

Mama was all sugar and politeness, asked him if he wouldn't like to take hisself a seat. Well, he didn't take the easy chair. Just set on the edge of the couch, perched.

They had a nice little chat. Leroy told her all about chickens, how they can see colors and smell blood. Mama said later on that he certainly was educational.

"He wasn't very nice to me, Hertz, and Truman," I had to put in.

"He don't tolerate no nonsense," she said.

———

Ordinarily I liked talking to guests of Annabelle, but Leroy was just not my sort. One time when him and Mama was at it, Leroy a-telling her about Rise'n'Shine being the number one chicken processor in southwestern Ohio, I got so bored I walked out to the kitchen looking for something to eat. I opened up the refrigerator, found the fudge I'd burnt the night before. I took the pan, chiseled me a piece, and walked back out to the living room.

"Want a piece of fudge?" I said to Leroy.

"Oh, Mary Mae, you shouldn't be offering that," Mama said. "It's burnt."

"If it's fudge, I'd like a piece," he said, giving me a wink. Only time he was nice to me was when Mama was in the room.

I handed it to him.

He took the whole thing, put it down in a single bite. "Delicious," he said.

"Oh, you're just being polite," Mama said.

"No, Mrs. Krebs, I like fudge."

Leroy was so bent on being polite to Mama he had no taste at all.

ANNABELLE

Soon's Leroy left that first time he was over, I begun making up a song.

LEROY'S A PUMPKIN, LEROY'S A DREAD.
GOTTA GET LEROY OUTTA MY HEAD.

That's all I could think of, but I kept singing it over and over to myself.

I was wishing Annabelle would give Leroy the heave-ho and just go out with Earl C. Hubbard. Earl C. was nice. She'd met him at a flea market. He'd come by about seven-thirty on a Friday or Saturday night. Annabelle, she'd be upstairs getting dressed, so she'd say, "Mary Mae, why don't you get the door?"

I didn't mind. Earl C. was always in jeans and a plaid shirt, and he'd set hisself down in the easy chair, the one with the flowers, and he'd say, "How you doing, Mary Mae?"

"Me, I'm doing fine," I'd say.

"You doing good in school? I bet you're smart."

"Yeah, I'm smart." Usually I left it at that, though one time I went and found him a test I'd took. Spelled Nebuchadnezzar perfect.

"Yep, I think I'll have you work for me. You know how to repair fences?" Earl C. worked at Hesselman Tool & Die in downtown Cincinnati, but he had a farm down in Kentucky, just outside Republic, about thirty miles north of Somerset. Warn't a big farm, he said, just fifty acres and an old log cabin he was putting electric into.

"Nope," I said, "never repaired fences."

"I bet you could learn real quick. How about baling hay? You know how to bale hay?"

"Nope."

"Bet you could learn that, too."

We'd go back and forth, him and me, him asking me could I do this, could I do that, me saying no, I didn't know how, and him saying he bet I could learn.

Mama would come in and say, "What you two carrying on about?" And Earl C. would josh with her for a while.

Mama liked Earl C. well enough. She said she thought he was a decent man, but she didn't like it the way he'd come in, set right down in the easy chair, and make hisself at home.

"A person shouldn't be too comfortable in someone else's house," she'd say after he'd left with Annabelle.

I thought maybe that was one of them verses out of the Bible like "Be ye kind one to another." But Daddy said it was just something Mama made up. It was her reason for not liking Earl C.

Thing is, I liked Annabelle. Her room was right across from mine. She said I could come in anytime I wanted, just knock. She would be in jeans and a sweatshirt, setting in her chair by the window a-working on a quilt square. Her hair was short and natural curly. I thought she was real pretty.

I'd come by and say, "I got a new song. Want to hear it?"

She always did. I sung her all the songs I made up and the ones I'd learned from my great-granny. That's where I got my guitar. My great-granny left it to me when she died. That and a whole box full of music—songs she'd wrote herself and songs she had the words for.

Annabelle would listen to me, and I mean really listen. Not like Mama and Daddy, that was always doing something else at the same time. She'd say at the end of a song, "Now what was that line about the sparrow? I liked that." Sometimes after I'd gone through a song a couple of times, she'd join in. And then she'd say, "Mary Mae, you got you a gift."

She meant it, too. She said I was lucky that I could sing and play. "What do you think you're going to do with your music?" Annabelle asked me one day.

"I want to write songs," I said. "And I want to write a book about my great-granny's music. She could play just about any instrument—banjo, guitar, fiddle, dulcimer. And she sung on a radio show every Saturday night, *The Hidey Mountain Holler*

Show. I want to go right down there to where she lived, in Crawdad in eastern Kentucky, and talk to everybody that knowed her." Crawdad was near Bitter Creek, where I was born. Great-Granny was my mama's granny.

"You got a purpose. Now me, I don't know what I'm doing."

"You got quilts," I said.

"Yeah, I got quilts, and they give me a lot of pride. But I don't do nothing but make them. You got a plan."

That was true. Me, eleven, knowed what I wanted better than Annabelle, that was twenty-one.

I was lucky, I guess. My great-granny showed me a lot of things before she died. Like how to play a dulcimer. I was too little to hold a guitar, so she give me a dulcimer. On a mountain dulcimer, you don't have to work but one string to get you a tune. The other two is drones. So I learned on that, and started making up my own songs, and always knowed I wanted to make music.

But Annabelle, her daddy died when she was

six, and her mama died last year. She come up to Cincinnati in a Honda with a little U-Haul attached. Made the hundred-and-fifty-mile trip on a Saturday by herself. She said she come across the Ohio River into Cincinnati, found a newspaper with our ad in it, called Mama, and drove on into DeSailles, which is not too far from downtown.

Annabelle had planned on staying at a motel until she found a place to live, but Mama said she could move right in. We even helped her unload her U-Haul. Then she got herself a job at Rise'n'Shine, started dating Earl C. and, later, Leroy. Everything seemed to be going real well for Annabelle, but sometimes she seemed lost.

"You think I should take that class in accounting?" she asked.

"Yes, Annabelle, I think you're real smart. I seen you add up them numbers." One time I seen her add a column half a page long, all double digits. She run up that page and back down faster than a squirrel with a head for numbers.

"Think I should get married?"

That was what I liked about Annabelle, asking

me questions like that. Growed-up questions about jobs and boyfriends and what she should wear. None of them other ladies we had living with us asked me questions like that. Just kept to themselves with the door shut. Course they didn't have boyfriends or quilts.

"Yes, Annabelle, I think you should get married. But only if it's to Earl C."

SHIRLEY WHIRLY

Problem is, Mama begun asking Earl C. personal questions.

"Is there much money in tool and die?" she asked him one night.

"Enough to keep me going," Earl C. said.

"What do you raise down there on that farm?"

"Sometimes I raise *cane*," he said, laughing, though Mama didn't get the joke. "Corn and hay, mostly."

I told Annabelle later on that Mama ought to mind her own business.

"She's just looking out for me, Mary Mae," she said, "and I appreciate her concern."

But I was concerned for Annabelle, too.

There's this girl at school, Shirley Whirly. She set behind me, and she was always tapping me on the back telling me stuff. One day, she tapped me on the back real excited and said, "Guess what? My sister Sallie Ann's a-getting married and I'm to be a junior bridesmaid."

"Your sister?" I said. "How old is she?"

"Nineteen."

"She got a ring?" I asked.

"Yep," Shirley said, and then she told me how Odelle, her sister's boyfriend, proposed. "They was up at Eden Park looking out on the river. Just a-setting in Odelle's car. And he reached around to the backseat and give her this little white box from the bakery. Sallie Ann opened it up and there was a cupcake with a lot of whipped cream on it. And he told her, 'Eat it real careful.' So she did, and what do you know, she found her ring in the icing. Ain't that sweet?"

"Yes," I said. "That was real sweet."

Every day Shirley was a-telling me the latest about the wedding, about her sister's dress and her junior bridesmaid dress and how they was getting white gloves and white hose, and how they went out and tried things on, and one day she up and says, "You got to come over. I want to show you my dress."

Usually I went home after school and messed around with Hertz and Truman until Mama got home. She's a bookkeeper at Harbin Plumbing. Then I'd go in and do homework. But Mama told me before I left for school I could go over to Shirley's if I got home by five.

So me and Shirley walked to her house together. She lived in a shotgun house on Broom Street just behind the Wertzheimer Furniture Factory. Shirley and her sister shared a bedroom, and her mama and daddy slept on a sofa-sleeper in the living room. Nobody was home. Shirley got us a Coca-Cola and some soda crackers, and then she showed me the dresses, all wrapped up in plastic, and hanging in their bedroom closet. Sallie Ann's bride dress was sleeveless, with embroidered flowers and pearls (Shirley called them mother-of-pearl) around the neckline. Then she showed me her junior brides-maid dress, all in pink satin with puffed sleeves.

"Nice," I said. "Big puffed sleeves." Though I wouldn't never want to wear sleeves like that. I'd feel silly.

"Mama says you got to do it right. You only get married once, she said. Or you're only supposed to. And look at this." Shirley opened up the door to a little glass cupboard. "All these presents Odelle give her." A little palm tree that turned on a pedestal and sung "Love Me Tender." A cup with *Sallie Ann* on it. A stuffed bear with a red neckerchief. "And she only just met Odelle last year."

Shirley shut the door to the cupboard, then she got some big, thick magazines down from a shelf—*Bride*, *Modern Bride*, *Christian Bride*, all of them bursting with yellow stickums. We took them into the living room, and Shirley begun showing me her favorite dresses.

"I want me one with roses and embroidered scallops," Shirley said.

"You mean for *your* wedding?" It seemed odd, her talking about *her* wedding.

"Sure. What kind of dress do you want?"

Well, I hadn't never thought about it. But I thumbed through and finally said, "Me, I just want to have a long white robe, like an intergalactic princess." That was the truth. I didn't like any of them dresses. They was all too fussy.

"Princess?" said Shirley. "Hm." She cocked her head like as if to say, Well, some people was pretty loony.

I was beginning to wish I hadn't come over. I didn't like bride magazines, and I didn't like soda crackers. Then Shirley flipped on the TV to a soap opera. I didn't like soap operas, neither. "You watch this all the time?" I asked.

"*Eternal Storm*?" said Shirley. "Never miss it. I think Tad should marry Lydia, but he's engaged to Simone, and, anyway, Lydia's taking off for the Bahamas to make jewelry from sand dollars."

All this mess made me think of Annabelle, her going out with Leroy one night and Earl C. the next. I watched *Eternal Storm* until Lydia boarded her plane for the Bahamas, then I said I had to go. Shirley said, "You should stay 'til the end. Your mama wouldn't mind if you was a little bit late."

"No, I got to get home," I said.

Hertz and Truman was setting on my front porch, wondering where I'd been. "You missed the dead possum," Truman said.

"Yeah, right out by the streetlight," said Hertz. "City Disposal just took it away."

"So?" I said. I went inside. Wished I'd seen it. Wished I'd come straight home.

That night I went to bed wishing Leroy would take off for the Bahamas, and Earl C. would move in quick with a few presents and a ring.

KITCHEN CHATS

But Mama begun having more and more chats with Annabelle down in the kitchen. Usually they started out talking about quilts or hairdos, but mostly they ended up talking about men. Annabelle was beginning to listen to Mama more than me—I guess because she thought Mama knowed more. Annabelle would say something like "I just don't know."

And Mama, she'd come over to the table a-working in some hand lotion, and would say, "Just don't know about what?"

I'd be setting down at the other end of the table with my guitar. Pretending I was writing up some songs, strumming a note here and there, but listening to every word.

"Oh, you know."

"Leroy and Earl C.?"

"Hmmmm—"

"Are they putting the pressure on?"

"You might say that."

And then Mama set down and just let Annabelle spill the beans, Mama trying real hard not to sound too nosy or too pushy, but getting in there all the same. "Well, what are they saying?"

"Oh, Earl C., he wants me to spend more time with him, get down to his farm on Saturdays—"

"Oh?" said Mama. She put her elbows on the table and set her chin on her hands. You could tell she was settling in for a nice, juicy session.

But right then, Daddy come through the kitchen with a curtain rod on his head. It was a short one, with a curtain on each side. Made him look like an Egyptian pharaoh. He didn't say nothing, just walked through.

Me and Annabelle started laughing.

Mama set right up. "Farley, you got better hats you can wear."

Daddy done that because he was trying to bust up the chat and get Mama to mind her own business. But Mama was on the scent. She wouldn't let up for nothing. "Go on," she said to Annabelle.

"But then Leroy, he wants me to spend Saturdays with him—"

"Well, Annabelle, I think at this time of your life you got to be thinking about who you want to settle down with."

"Yes—" Annabelle was sort of embarrassed.

"And you got to consider who would be a good provider."

I couldn't help but interrupt. "She's providing for herself," I said. I thought Mama ought to get with the times.

But Annabelle was listening to Mama. "Oh, I think they would both be good providers."

You could tell Mama didn't agree with that. "Well, let's see. Earl C.'s a tool-and-die man. And he knows farming. Yes, he could provide. But how well? Where's he going? You compare him to Leroy. There's a man that's a-going places. He's selling chicken parts and already been named assistant manager."

"So?" I said. "Earl C.'s planning on opening up a repair shop down in Republic."

"Well, I haven't heard about it," Mama said, as if it couldn't be true because Earl C. hadn't told her. But he warn't one to brag. "Besides," Mama said, coming in from another angle, "do you really want to end up in a log cabin?"

"I wouldn't mind," Annabelle said. She said it sort of quiet and hesitant, then added, in an even smaller voice, "He's electrifying it."

"But is that where you want to spend the rest of your life? Is that where you want your kids raised?" asked Mama.

Annabelle was afraid to answer, so I answered for her. "I'd like to live in a log cabin," I said. I could just picture it. Me with my guitar and Hertz. We would be mountain people with our own vegetable patch.

Now Mama, she grew up in a cabin on Bitter Creek, and she didn't like it. Couldn't wait to get out, she used to say. So when I was two, Daddy moved us up to DeSailles.

"Annabelle," Mama said, "you want to be near

supermarkets and a Drive-Thru Dairy Barn." She thumped the table on "Dairy Barn," then added, real confidential, "You want to be in the city with a man that can buy you things."

"Cluck, cluck," I said.

"Mary Mae, I've had just about enough of you." Mama was barreling in and didn't want no interference. "You know, if I was you, Annabelle, I'd set my cap for Leroy."

"Leroy?" Annabelle said.

"Yes, Annabelle, I got to tell you I think Leroy's a man of promise. Won that Rise'n'Shine award for selling the most chicken parts."

"Yes," Annabelle said, "he does win awards."

"Yes, and I think he can hold his own in a conversation." Mama loved the way he talked facts and figures with her.

"I suppose."

"Annabelle, you want you a good provider. And I can tell you that if I was in your shoes, Leroy would be my man."

Annabelle set there nodding.

I just wanted to shake Annabelle—listening

to my mama the way she done. I strummed a little tune. Wanted to slow this whole thing down.

"Oh yes, Leroy is the man for you." And then she threw in the clincher. "Why, he worships the ground you walk on."

Annabelle's face suddenly glowed, as if this was the nicest thing she'd ever heard. "Do you think so?" You could tell that bells was going off in Annabelle's head.

I stopped playing. Warn't no use now.

The problem with Mama telling Annabelle who to choose was Mama just never did seem to know what was what. Except for choosing Daddy, she had terrible taste in men. For instance, down at Remnant—that's our church, Remnant Church of God—there was these two boys Mama thought was real spiffy. "Oh, that Jonathan Safer, he knows his Bible," she'd said to me one Sunday.

"Yes, and he has green teeth," I had said.

"Well, what about Chester Morley? Has two

paper routes and helps his mama count the collection."

"You never seen the way he chases girls around the parking lot and pins them up against the fence."

"Chester Morley?"

"Besides, he walks like a penguin."

"Earl C.'s real nice, too," I said that day in the kitchen. But it was like as if they didn't hear me. So I added, "Leroy's a priss."

Mama raised her arm like she was about to swat. She hadn't swatted me since I was eight years old.

"That's it," Mama said. "You get upstairs."

"Cluck, cluck."

Christmastime, Leroy drug in a big old wooden chest. He brung it over, a-sticking out of the trunk of his Plymouth, this long chest with little feet like paws. I said to Mama, who was standing there with a chain of popcorn around her neck, "What's that?"

We was in the middle of putting up our tree.

"That there's a hope chest," she said. "It's an old-fashioned present, something a man gives a woman when he's thinking of asking her to marry." You could tell Mama thought it was about the dreamiest thing since Cool Whip.

So I knowed things was moving fast and there warn't much hope for Earl C. Fact is, he hadn't been around since Mama'd told Annabelle she should set her cap for Leroy.

Then Annabelle, she begun filling her hope chest with things she collected on her lunch hour— dish towels, napkins, a potato peeler, a hand vegetable slicer called the Julie-Ann.

One night she come home with a shiny round dish with little places for deviled eggs. "Ain't this cute?" she said. "I picked this up at Corliss Hardware."

"Yep, that's a dandy," Mama said. "I wish I had me one of them."

One day when I was in Annabelle's room, I just out and said, "Annabelle, you said you had a better time with Earl C. Why don't you go out with him no more?"

"I did have a nice time with Earl C.," she said real slow, "but I need me a man that's rising high in the company."

VALENTINE'S DAY

So I warn't that surprised what happened on Valentine's Day.

Mama, she made a special meal of pork chops and gravy. But Annabelle was late. Mama kept drumming her fingers on the Formica, saying, "Well, where is that girl? It's six-thirty and she ain't here. It's polite to call."

"Maybe she's out with Leroy," I said, thinking that might cheer her up.

"That might be true, but certainly Leroy would have the good manners to let us know if they was going to be late."

Hertz gave me some red guitar picks for Valentine's Day, and I gave him and Truman some candy hearts. I knowed Leroy would get Annabelle something big, but I was hoping just a box of chocolates.

Well, we was all in the dining room, and Daddy had just said the blessing when we heard Annabelle's key in the door. Around the corner she come and set down in her coat. You could tell she was about to burst with something, keeping her lips sealed tight to keep from smiling. She let her pocketbook slide off her arm onto the floor. Then she unbuttoned her coat, pulled her left hand out of her sleeve, and held it over the gravy.

There it was—a diamond.

"We was having coffee at Billie's Diner," she said. "He took it out of his pocket, held it up for the waitress to see first, and said, 'Got a present for my gal.' Then he blew off some lint and put it on my finger."

"Oh, Lord," Mama said, "ain't that beautiful."

"It's just a little bitty one," Annabelle said. "We're saving up for a refrigerator." She sounded like she already knowed she was getting a ring.

"I think you're wise," said Daddy. "Them refrigerators is expensive."

I put my nose down close to Annabelle's hand. "Looks like a sugar crystal to me," I said.

"Mary Mae!" Mama said. "You ought to say 'Congratulations.' "

I said it, but I didn't mean it. Leroy warn't the man for Annabelle. She was too nice for him.

"When's the big day?" asked Daddy.

"June first," said Annabelle. "I always wanted to be a June bride. And you'll be my junior bridesmaid," she said to me.

"Well, ain't that nice," Mama said.

"Me?" I said. Oh my. Annabelle was looking at me so expectant, I didn't dare refuse. Even though I didn't want her marrying Leroy, I couldn't let Annabelle down.

I told Hertz and Truman about Annabelle the next day when we was walking over to Little Lukey's in the snow, but they warn't no help.

Truman started making little smooching sounds.

Hertz said, "Maybe he'll beat her up," and he grabbed Truman and they went rolling into a snowbank.

———

I talked to Daddy, too. After the snow melted, we went out fishing off a bridge on the Little Miami. "It's Mama that talked Annabelle into marrying Leroy," I said.

"When Mama is determined, sometimes there ain't nothing you can do but get out of the way," he said.

"But she's ruining Annabelle's life." I felt real growed-up saying that, like as if I was older than Mama.

"Mama don't see it that way," Daddy said. "She's just giving advice. Her best advice. It's her way of showing love."

But I wanted to show love, too. "I'll tell Annabelle that Mama's wrong."

"Mary Mae, you can't write someone else's life. You got to admit Annabelle seems to like Leroy. She's got to live her life her own way. Even if it means marrying a cock of the walk." There it was. He out and said it. Admitted what Leroy was. Then Daddy was quiet for a while, baiting up another hook. "Maybe Annabelle needs to learn to be a better judge of people."

So I knowed right then what I had to do—help Annabelle to see Leroy for what he was.

At school, Shirley Whirly poked me in the back. "You should see the bouquet I'm going to carry," she said. "Me and Sallie Ann just went to the florist and picked out all the flowers. Sallie Ann's carrying white roses with calla lilies and the bridesmaids is carrying white tulips and pink roses with little bunches of lavender forget-me-nots."

I could have bragged right there, but I didn't. Didn't say one thing. I was just a-hoping Annabelle would give back Leroy's ring.

LITTLE LUKEY

Just as much as I hated Leroy, I loved Little Lukey. He was the boy with the heart murmur, lived on the first floor of a big old three-story. He was two and had hair the color of mayonnaise. You'd never know to look at him he had a hole in his heart. His mama and daddy wanted to have an operation on him before he turned three. Problem is, they didn't have enough money.

Mrs. Chassoldt done window displays for the DeSailles Discount Outlet. She didn't want to take a full-time job because she was afraid of leaving Lukey for too long. I'd go down there and babysit every Thursday from three 'til Mr. Chassoldt got home from work, usually around five-thirty.

One day toward the end of February, Mrs. Chassoldt was in her white blouse and jumper, getting ready to take off. "Mary Mae," she said, "Lukey's been a-looking forward to you coming in." She always said that, but today she had a worried look on her face.

After she left, I picked Little Lukey up out of his high chair—he was the cutest thing, wore corduroy overalls and a turtleneck shirt and had crumbs all around his mouth.

The Chassoldts didn't have much furniture, only some kitchen chairs and an old couch Mrs. Chassoldt picked up at the Outlet. And a braided rug just big enough for me and Lukey to play on. Mrs. Chassoldt had his toys out there on the floor.

We built a tower, then run some little cars around. Then I put him on my lap and sung him a song. It's one I made up. I'd get Lukey to clap and bounce him while I sang.

I CLAP MY HANDS,

I KICK MY FEET,

I RIDE MY HORSEY

ROUND.

MY HORSEY'S NAME IS
MARY MAE.
SHE TAKES ME INTO
TOWN.

GIDDYUP, GIDDYUP,
GIDDYUP, LET'S GO
LET'S RIDE THIS HORSEY
ROUND.

SHE GALLOPS THROUGH
THE WOODS WITH ME.
SHE TAKES ME
INTO TOWN.

He'd get real excited when I sung that song, and I was about to sing him another one, but Mr. Chassoldt come home early. "I thank you kindly, Mary Mae, but you can go on home," he said.

He paid me for my time, but he looked worried just like Mrs. Chassoldt had.

"Anything wrong, Mr. Chassoldt?" I said.

"We're having a little trouble at work."

Later Mama told me that Hasenour Bottling

Works, the company Mr. Chassoldt worked for, was laying off workers. "That ain't good, especially with them needing that operation for Lukey."

I told Hertz and Truman about Mr. Chassoldt and Little Lukey.

"Wish't we could do something for them," Hertz said. We was out in front of my house and it was real cold.

"Yeah, me too," said Truman.

"Like make money or something—them Chassoldts need money bad," I said.

All up and down Charter Avenue, stores had tin cans with slots on the top and a photograph of Little Lukey taped on. They was put there by the De-Sailles Boosters Club, but Mama heard they'd only collected about thirty dollars.

"Maybe we could sell something," Truman said.

"Nothing I can think of would make enough money," I said.

We went over to Hertz's house. His mama and daddy was divorced and his mama had moved to

Las Vegas. Hertz and his daddy lived in this house that was going to be torn down for an apartment, so Hertz could do just about anything he wanted. He could roller-skate and he could color up the walls. Hertz's daddy, Seymour, played lead guitar in a band, so his living room was full of guitars and speakers. When Seymour was around, he'd show me a few licks on the guitar.

Mama said he ought to get a real job, that playing music wasn't work. The way I see it, playing music's fun, but it's hard work, too.

Me and Hertz made us some cookie dough—stirred up the Betty Crocker chocolate chip mix, only we didn't bake it, just ate it by the spoonful—and then we watched TV, this show about kids that comes on every Tuesday. We heard the announcer tell about how these kids down in Florida made all this money for another kid by having a carnival. They planned it real good. Put out announcements, got everybody on their street into it, got booths, had a talent show, all that stuff.

So right away, we was each looking at the other, and we all said, "Let's have us a carnival."

We wanted to do it right away. We went over to Truman's house, come in through the back door. We started to make up some announcements on the kitchen table. But Mrs. Earlywine come in and said this was no overnight affair. If we wanted to make money, we had to plan it and do it right. We'd have to give the neighbors plenty of notice, she said, and she advised doing it on Memorial Day weekend. "That way it'll be nice and warm, and you'll collect a good crowd."

So Truman started carrying on. "That's three whole months away! I don't want to wait!" And he went banging around the kitchen, kicking chairs and slamming drawers. Sometimes he acts like he's two instead of nine.

Mrs. Earlywine's got a beauty shop in the front of the house, Corinne's Creations, what used to be the front porch, and there was ladies setting there in curlers could hear every word. Mrs. Earlywine was following him around the kitchen saying, "Now Truman, now Truman."

I'll tell you right here it was Mrs. Earlywine's own fault Truman acted the way he did. His daddy was dead and Truman's brother was twenty-five, so she just spoiled Truman to death. Give him a fifty-dollar bill one time for helping her clean out the cellar.

Truman's real generous, though. Treated me and Hertz to a pizza down at Bobo's Italian and then ordered a limo to take us home. You should have seen the neighbors when we pulled up in front of Truman's. Thinking we was all spoiled brats.

Anyway, me, being the most sensible of us three, I said, "All right, let's just make some posters and find out who wants to help."

"Now that's the way to do it," said Mrs. Early-wine.

Truman kicked one more cabinet, then simmered down.

"I'll get us some booths and tables from down at the association," Mrs. Earlywine said. Her owning her own business, she's a secretary or something for the Women's Business Association.

We all got around her typewriter and made our poster:

CAPP STREET CARNIVAL
for
LUKEY CHASSOLDT

The Little Kid with the HEART MURMUR

Saturday, May 25

Looking for Volunteers

Can you Sell Something?

Run a Booth?

Can you make a Special Food and Sell it?

Do you have Talent?

Would you like to be in Our Show?

Fill this out and return to the Earlywines,

623, or the Krebses, 621.

Name_____

Address_____

Later, down at the association, Mrs. Earlywine run it off on some paper, color of mustard, and we walked around sticking it behind everybody's screen door. Then we went around to the sides of houses to make sure we got the people that lived upstairs.

"Wonder how many's going to help us out?" Truman asked when we went back to my house with the leftover posters.

Mama was just coming home from work and she said, "What are you up to?"

We told her. She tossed her keys into the sky and let them drop on the cement. "Mary Mae, on June first Annabelle's a-getting married. Now, we can't have no carnival and wedding a-going on a week apart."

"Why not?"

"It's just too much."

"But Lukey needs the money."

Mama twisted her mouth off to one side and sniffed. That's what she does when she don't see the sense in something. I knowed she didn't like it that I hadn't asked her first. But I also knowed she would have told me we couldn't have it.

Hertz said, "You mean you don't love Little Lukey?"

"Of course I love Little Lukey," Mama said, picking up her keys. And you could see she thought better of saying more.

Tell you the truth, I don't know why grownups can't handle more than one event in a week. You just go to one, then you just go to the other.

"What do you want to do for the carnival?" I asked. "Do you want to make popcorn balls?" Mama was the only one I knowed who could make them nice and round.

"Well, I could," she said, "or some pawpaw cookies." Mama loved making them cookies. She still had plenty of canned pawpaws from when we went picking them down in the country last fall.

"Make both," I said.

Mama rolled her eyes and walked into the house.

Me, Hertz, and Truman went over to tell the Chassoldts. All Mrs. Chassoldt could do when she heard was cry. Mr. Chassoldt was saying, "Ain't that a wonderful thing. God bless." Lukey, he was in his high chair, tomato soup smeared all over his face and just a-kicking away.

Mrs. Chassoldt told me I wouldn't have to babysit no more for Lukey since Mr. Chassoldt was home Thursday afternoons. She was looking for more jobs dressing windows.

Next day, we was already getting notes and letters in our mailboxes. Ernest Childers, he said he could have his trained parrot walk through a ring of fire for the variety show, and Dotty Fortress, she was a-going to make them caramel apples, and Priscilla Widely, she'd sell heart-shaped pillows that she made herself, and two sisters down the street, Janice and Loretta Nonesuch, said they'd belly dance. They learned how to at the Y in their Take Off Weight Sensibly class. Verlie Wickoff said she would twirl fire batons.

Otis and Fay Portion said they'd make up their special chili in a big tub by the street. Percy Macon and her sister Sue was making and selling them cornhusk dolls. Then we'd have funnel cakes being made by Waylon Otter. He said he could get hisself a deep-fry from down at the rental place he worked at. Mavis Truffle said she *would* jump out of a plane in her parachute except she wasn't sure she could make it to landing on Capp Street. She was afraid of getting tangled up in them telephone wires, so she'd just bring her gear and show how to put it on and take it off.

Annabelle would be running a booth selling lots of stuff made by the ladies at work. They all said they could whip up some nice things on their lunch hour—pot holders, little crocheted coin purses, and handbags knit from thick yarn. Annabelle was going to raffle off a quilt she intended to make.

Mama told me to be careful if I had Annabelle doing anything. "She's sometimes not dependable," Mama said. I knowed what she was talking about. Annabelle was always late and putting things off 'til the last minute. But them quilts was to Annabelle what singing was to me. It was her gift. And I knowed she wanted to give.

Me, Hertz, and Truman was planning on doing a song for Little Lukey. And Mrs. Earlywine said I ought to do a solo as well. "Do something real special," she said. So I thought maybe I could take one of my great-granny's tunes and sing it. Cleon Riddle said he'd emcee the whole thing. He used to give Gray Line bus tours, so we knowed he'd do a good job.

Hertz's daddy said he'd bring his band over and they'd play for an hour before the show, just to warm up the crowd.

Mrs. Earlywine called up the police and asked them to block off Capp Street for the event, plus she got Channel Two News to cover it.

We put posters up in all the stores around town, and got triangular flags strung from rope to hang from the telephone poles. We put all that stuff down in Truman's cellar.

I tell you, even people that seen us come home in that limo and always thought we was up to no good was telling us what a wonderful thing we was doing, so we was all walking around with halos.

Leroy and Annabelle was setting in the living room one night. I come in and set down on the easy chair. Sometimes I said to myself, Maybe you're not being fair to Leroy, maybe he's not as bad as you think, you ought to give him one more chance.

So that's what was going through my mind when I asked him. "Leroy," I said, trying to sound real growed-up, "we're having a carnival to collect money for Little Lukey. He's that little kid down the street that's got a heart murmur. Would you like to help out?" I handed him one of our posters.

He looked it over, not saying nothing.

"Annabelle's making a quilt to raffle off," I said.

Leroy stood up. "A quilt." He laughed. "Well, she ought to be working on her cooking, not sewing them little squares together." He said this with a wink to Mama, who had just poked her head around the corner.

And then Annabelle said, "You could help me out, sell some chances for the raffle."

"Nah," he said, like his big-deal self, "I'll just come and spend money."

Later on, I said to Annabelle, "You know, if Leroy was my boyfriend, I'd want him to help."

"He's got a lot going on at Rise'n'Shine," said Annabelle.

But that night I started thinking about my Leroy song again.

> LEROY'S A PUMPKIN, LEROY'S A DREAD,
>
> GOTTA GET LEROY OUTTA MY HEAD.
>
> HE'S A BROWN SUIT, CLUCK-CLUCK,
>
> MR. PRISS, RISE'N'SHINE,
>
> LEROY. THAT'S LEROY.

I stopped right there. Got stuck.

RISE'N'SHINE

Shirley Whirly went on a-bragging about all the doings at her sister's wedding. How they was all going to the Oddfellows Hall afterward for a big party with a real band. Slim and His Pickin's. And how they was going to have chicken Parmesan, whatever that was. I'd listen to her and never say a word about Annabelle. Still just hoped Annabelle would up and put that ring back in Leroy's pocket.

But one day when Shirley Whirly was a-bragging about the dyed-to-match shoes she was to wear, I couldn't hold back no longer. "I'm going to be a junior bridesmaid, too," I said. "June first."

"Oh?" said Shirley. You could tell she was sort of disappointed, not being the *only* girl in class to be a bridesmaid. "Whose wedding?"

"Annabelle's. Our boarder's."

"Well, what are you wearing?"

"We ain't picked it out yet," I said. I told her about the pictures Annabelle had pinned up all over her room, and how we had yet to go shopping.

"She better hurry up. You're supposed to have your dress picked out six months before." Shirley Whirly was real smug, like she knowed everything.

"Annabelle's more worried about her silver pattern," I said. I just had to show Shirley I knowed as much about weddings as she did.

"What's a silver pattern?"

"The kind of forks and spoons you want to have."

Then she warmed up real quick. "We're lucky, ain't we, being bridesmaids? When you get your dress, you got to invite me over."

"Sure will." And then my stomach begun to clench and I was thinking to myself, What kind of a person are you, Mary Mae? You don't want Annabelle to marry Leroy, but you're a-bragging about being in her wedding.

Ever since I'd been to Shirley's and been listening to all this wedding talk, I couldn't help but think what kind of wedding I'd want to have. I liked things that was different. I wanted to have it on the top of an Indian mound and I'd be wearing my intergalactic princess gown. We'd have a medicine man do the ceremony. And then afterward we'd have a feast at a long table with roast beef sandwiches, taco chips, and six kinds of dip.

I expected I would marry Hertz, though I never told nobody, not even Hertz. We wouldn't live in no regular house, but a cabin built up against the mountain. We'd have a recording studio in it, though we'd go off to town in a red pickup for performances. Sometimes I would sing alone, and Hertz, he would stay at home and work on computers. That's what he liked better than singing.

Annabelle asked me one night did I want to go over to Rise'n'Shine with her and Leroy. They was getting ready for their Spring Chicken Bonanza and Leroy had some papers to file. She said we could probably get him to take me through the plant. Ever since Annabelle had started work there, I'd always wanted to see what they done with them chickens.

We come in through the side entrance marked "Employees Only," and Leroy had us put on hairnets and little earplugs. Leroy looked like a chicken hisself in one of them hairnets, and I tried not to look at him so I could keep from laughing. All the people on the night shift, mostly women, was wearing the same hairnets and earplugs we was. The machines was mighty loud. Leroy yelled out to me over the noise, "This here's where they come after they've had their feathers took off!" There was all these birds dangling upside down, just a-coming around on a conveyor over our heads, naked and their necks swinging.

"How do they get their feathers took off?" I yelled back.

Leroy took a quick breath as if to say, Why are you making all this work for me? But he took us into the next room. Them upside-down birds was passing between two long lines of little wormy things. Leroy said them wormy things was called "rubber fingers." They was just a-beating them feathers right off.

"How do they get hung by their feet?" I asked.

"You don't want to see that," said Leroy.

"Yes, I do," I said.

And then Annabelle chimed in behind me, "Yes, I think Mary Mae should see that." I was proud to hear Annabelle a-speaking up to Leroy.

"Okay, follow me," he said. We walked back to another part of the plant. He said, "Watch your step," and opened a door. It was dark, except for some red lights. Leroy said chickens couldn't see in red light. Them chickens was being brought in off a truck, not squawking much but real startled-looking, and men was putting their legs in the "shackles." That's what Leroy said them little stirrups was called. Leroy said they got their throats slit in the next room and that they didn't feel nothing.

I thought he was probably right. Once them birds was hanging from the shackles, they was all pretty peaceful.

We went over to the other side of the plant to the package room, and all them birds was coming off cut and ready in little yellow trays with plastic over the top, and that's when I got me an idea.

"Leroy," I said, thinking if he could do this for us, I might could think a little better of him, "how about for the carnival Rise'n'Shine donating some of them chickens? Or giving out some coupons people could use at the store? You could even have your own booth."

Well, Leroy, he stopped, put his hand against the wall, looked up, looked down, pulled his hairnet off. "Mary Mae, Rise'n'Shine don't have no time to get involved in no kiddy carnival."

"Why not?" asked Annabelle. She was not only a-speaking up to Leroy tonight but giving him some back talk.

"We're not in the carnival business. We got a bottom line to meet. Can't be giving to no charity."

So that was that.

But I walked down the hall just a-humming that Leroy song in my head, and adding to it as I went.

LEROY'S A PUMPKIN, LEROY'S A DREAD,

GOTTA GET LEROY OUTTA MY HEAD.

HE'S A BROWN SUIT, CLUCK-CLUCK,

MR. PRISS, RISE'N'SHINE
UP-AND-COMER, WHEELER-DEALER,
CHICKEN PARTS A-GOING PLACES—
LEROY, THAT'S LEROY.

We went into Leroy's office. He had his name on the door, Leroy Cuzzens, Assistant Manager. He was picking up different stacks of paper and moving them around on the desk, just showing off how much work he had to do. Me and Annabelle pulled our hairnets off, dropped our earplugs into Leroy's wastebasket.

I took a look at the books on his desk—*The Power Man's Business Book*, *How to Keep Your Employees in Line*, *Wheeling and Dealing*, and a big thick one, *Chicken Management, Pure and Simple*. But that warn't all that was in his office. He had a punching bag and a big old orange chicken, a real one, stuffed, wearing a blue-and-white checked apron and little bonnet. It was set up on a post and had a label around its neck, "Miss Rise'n'Shine."

"What's that for?" I asked Leroy.

"That's my prize for selling the most chicken parts," he said. "Got it from Central Office. Thought I'd give it to Annabelle."

"To me?" Annabelle said. Her hands crossed her chest and her mouth dropped. You'd a-thought she'd been given the Medal of Honor.

"Thought since things was getting crowded here, you could keep it," he said.

Mama was so impressed with Miss Rise'-n'Shine she had Leroy leave it in front of the fireplace. "It's a work of art," she said.

WEDDING DRESS

Annabelle said the quilt she begun working on to raffle off at the carnival was called Birds in the Air. She showed me a picture of it in a book. There was triangles put together with triangles and all of them forming diamonds. If you squinted your eyes, it looked like a whole flock of birds, and you could almost hear them flapping. She was doing it in shades of pale blue and gold, pieces from some satin dust ruffles she picked up at a garage sale.

"This pattern looks hard," I said. "Think you can have it finished by the time of the carnival?" It was the end of March, and I remembered what Mama had said about Annabelle sometimes not being dependable.

"I'm determined," she said.

One day when me and Annabelle was up in her room and she was stitching away so content, I just out and asked her, "Annabelle, does Leroy write you love letters?"

"He slips me a note now and then," she said.

"About what?" I knowed Mama would be saying it was none of my business, but she would have wanted to know herself.

"He'll say something about maybe we should go up to Billie's Diner for lunch."

"That's all?" I said.

"That's about it."

"Don't he sign it, 'Love, Leroy'?"

"He spells it L-U-V."

"He ought to spell it right." I imagined getting love letters from Hertz. Sometimes he gave me notes in school, when my class was passing his. I was in sixth grade and he was in fifth.

MEET YOU AT KRAMER'S MARKET.

I GOT A DOLLAR. WE'LL GET SOME

PEPPERONI STIX.

The last Saturday in March, me and Annabelle went out shopping for her wedding dress. Annabelle wasn't sure where to go, but I told her, "Shirley Whirly's sister went to Ronda's Bride-Elle." I'd been telling Annabelle all about Shirley Whirly's sister's wedding.

"Ladies at work said that's a good store," said Annabelle. "Besides, they're having a sale."

So after taking a quick look at Bridetown USA, which was nearby, and thinking everything looked like it had been worn before, we ended up at Ronda's Bride-Elle, out Finley Farms Road. The shop was split up into two rooms, with tuxedos on one side and dresses on the other. The bride dresses was wrapped up in clear plastic bags, and they was hung around three sides of the room. Dresses for the bridesmaids, mostly in rainbow colors, was hung on some racks in the middle. There was a desk at the front and two chairs, and we set down with a woman in a real stiff hairdo. She said to Annabelle, "What can I help you ladies with?"

"I'm getting married in June," Annabelle said, "and I want me something in satin, long. I seen your ad for Spring Inventory."

"So, you're interested in dresses on sale?" the lady said. "I think we can find you something." She showed us a rack of nice dresses, all different kinds of white. Annabelle took five of them back to a little room and tried them on. One was too big in the shoulders. Another one had a matching headpiece with a point that come down into Annabelle's forehead so she looked like Dracula. Then she tried on what the lady called "Victorian." It was all pooched out in the back and had little bows at the wrist. Annabelle was afraid she wouldn't be able to set down. Next was something the lady said had a "mermaid silhouette," slinky-looking and too tight, with little buttons up the back, and that just warn't Annabelle.

Finally she put on this cream-colored satin dress with long sleeves and a sweetheart neckline. Just what she wanted, she said. She backed off from the mirror, checking herself out.

"What do you think of this one, Mary Mae?"

"Nice," I said. Too nice for Leroy, I thought to myself.

The lady in charge said she thought it ought to

be tighter in the waist and she pulled it a little in the back. "We can have that done," she said. She had a seamstress come out and put pins in the dress, promised to have it ready in a week.

Annabelle tried on a bunch of headpieces—one like a crown, another I thought looked like a Viking helmet, one that was just a bow, and another that looked like a nurse's cap. Man, was they expensive. Just a little bit of net and some seed pearls and they was charging you a hundred and fifty dollars. So I said to Annabelle, "You ought to go down to the DeSailles Discount Outlet. They got stuff like this for five dollars."

"Not for my wedding, I'm not," Annabelle said.

"It's the beading that costs," the woman said, and she pointed to the pearls that was sewn into the netting. She found another one without any beading, just a circle of flowers, for seventy-five dollars, and Annabelle said she'd take that.

Back in her jeans, Annabelle tried on the headpiece once more, just to make sure she liked it.

Then I tried on bridesmaid dresses. The rest of

the bridesmaids was to be friends from Annabelle's office. We was looking for something me and them would look nice in. I didn't want one like Shirley's, with big puffed sleeves. One the lady held up to me was a dark pink color, with this scooped neck, but Annabelle thought that looked too dark for a June wedding.

"I like pastel," said Annabelle. "That'll look nice on Mary Mae and everybody else, and be good for June."

So the lady, she give me these long dresses and I went and put them on and I tell you, some of them was really stupid-looking. One had a huge collar just like a shawl. The saleslady called that a "portrait collar." Another had little balls of fringe and scallops and I was scared to death I was going to have to wear something like that, but Annabelle pretty much felt the same way I did about what I was trying on. Finally, I put on a mint green dress that the lady called "princess style." The sleeves ended at my elbows. It fit perfect. When I walked out, Annabelle and the saleslady said, "That's the one."

The lady handed me a bouquet of fake yellow flowers.

Seeing how I looked, I was almost getting excited about the wedding. Or at least parading around somewhere in that outfit. Wait'll Shirley Whirly hears about this, I thought. I pulled my hair up. I bet I looked thirteen.

Annabelle said she'd send her other bridesmaids in and they could get measured, and meanwhile I could take my dress home in a plastic bag.

"What are you doing for footwear?" the lady asked. She pointed to a big display of white satin shoes. "We can have these dyed to match. We send them off to our main store and have them back in two weeks."

Annabelle wasn't sure.

"Shirley Whirly's getting dyed-to-match," I said.

Dyed-to-match it was.

We stopped at the mall on the way home, and Annabelle, she wanted to run through Lillian's Lingerie. There was all them mannequins with fancy underwear in the window like Annabelle had showed me in the back of them bridal magazines, and I said, "Are you getting special underwear?"

"Yes, that's part of my trousseau."

"What's a trousseau?"

"It's all the clothes a bride puts together for her marriage."

I'd have to ask Shirley Whirly if her sister had a trousseau. Me and Shirley was using all kinds of big words, like "fiancé" and "honeymoon" and "nuptials." I thought nuptials was a plant that growed in the garden, but Annabelle said no, it was the wedding ceremony.

She found her a yellow nightgown, all lace and slinky, and a matching robe. Picked them out, didn't even try them on.

After that, we got us a free chocolate at Just Desserts. They always have a little plate full of samples. Then we went into this game store that was playing a video. We was just moseying around. I don't know what movie was on, but there was this man and a woman and they was about to get married, but the woman didn't look too happy about it. She was standing on a front porch holding a little bouquet of flowers. And then this other man drove up in an old-time car with whitewall tires, climbed the steps onto the porch, and said, "You're not in love with him. It's me you want." And then he pulled her into his arms and give her this real long kiss.

I looked over at Annabelle. She was watching, but she didn't say nothing. Just moved on to magnifying glasses, which she tried out.

But that movie give me an idea. I'd call up Earl C. and get him to come to the carnival. Like I said, I believed in miracles.

Me and Annabelle went to the food court and got us a snack of bacon-lettuce-and-tomato sandwiches.

Annabelle said, "Leroy likes these. I should learn how to make them."

"Let him make them himself," I said.

"You don't like him, do you?"

I'd already told her that. "Mama's not always right, you know."

"But Leroy's a-going places."

"Where are you going? He don't even want you

taking accounting." I had heard him tell her she'd be wasting her money.

"He just said I don't have no head for figures."

"But you do. I seen you adding up them columns. And figuring out quilt patterns. You're real good. He should be helping you to see what you can do."

That's what Earl C. would have said. And Shirley Whirly said her sister's boyfriend wanted her sister to do whatever made her happy.

Annabelle didn't say nothing. She just put some more mayonnaise on her sandwich and we set there a-watching the orangeade machine.

DOWNTOWN

Once we got home, I took my dress and put it on. Stood out on the back porch feeling like a lady in a castle. Hertz and Truman, they was hanging off the old swing in Truman's backyard a-singing "Here Comes the Bride."

I stuck my tongue out, went inside, and changed.

I found Earl C.'s number in Annabelle's little book by the phone, but I was afraid if I called right then Annabelle might hear me.

Pretty soon Hertz and Truman was banging on my door.

"Was that your wedding dress?" Truman asked.

"I told you, I'm a junior bridesmaid," I said. "And I'm sick of weddings. Let's go downtown and get some boxes." Mrs. Earlywine said we needed them for the carnival, to put supplies in.

We got Truman's wagon. But we didn't start collecting right away.

We walked down to the Salvation Army, picked us all out a hat. You can get them for a dime on Saturdays, when all the stuff with yellow tags goes on sale. Hertz got hisself an army hat, and Truman, he got a good old coonskin, and me, I got a big red felt with a velvet bow glued onto the crown. Then we walked down Union to the De-Sailles Discount Outlet, picked us each out a kazoo, and went on down to the Wertzheimer Furniture Store.

We found a few boxes that had been knocked flat, leaning against the back of the building. We put them on the wagon, hid everything between the building and the Dumpster. Then we went inside and had us a parade. First we walked through Patio Furniture. We had our kazoos and we was just a-going with this song we all liked called "My Baby's Hot as Mustard Though It's Cold as Ice Out Thar." It's one we learned off a CD. We done a circle twice around this white table with an umbrella. Then we went on down to Beds & Mattresses. Hertz, he laid out on one called Firm, and Truman, he got hisself on a Soft, and I got myself on a Medium and we done our Three Bears routine.

"Someone's been sleeping in my bed," Hertz said.

"Hey," said Truman, "someone's been sleeping in my bed."

And I was a-bouncing away, and I said, "Well someone's been sleeping in my bed, too."

Pretty soon we was all standing up and bouncing and the salesman come over and told us to get out of there or he was calling the police.

So we moved on. Slow. Warn't no reason to go quick. We warn't doing nothing illegal. We went playing our kazoos, too. More of that "My Baby's Hot as Mustard . . ."

Outside, Truman got his wagon and we went on down to Corliss Hardware Store. It was one of our favorite places, across the street and in the new mall. You name it, they got it—mailboxes shaped like Conestoga wagons, plastic sleds, bells, gongs, screwdrivers with six heads, barbecues turning plastic legs of lamb, little bitty flashlights, and plungers big as your head.

We found a few more flat boxes, then tied the wagon with all the boxes on it to the bike rack. Then we went in playing our kazoos, just having a good old time.

Truman said, "What are them cameras for?" He was looking up over his head at the TV camera hanging from the ceiling.

Hertz said, "You don't know? Them's for watching the people, seeing if there's any shop-lifters."

"Yeah," I said. "I seen it on TV once. There's this man that sits in a little room with all these screens and he's just a-keeping his eye on every-body."

"Yeah?" said Truman, and he started pacing around, doing his gorilla imitation. Well then, Hertz, he decided he'd do a hoedown like he done with his daddy's band, and me, I was singing "Don't Be Passing Corn to Me If You're Still Deep in Mud," which was one of my great-granny's old songs. Me in my red felt hat, just a-singing like I was onstage.

Pretty soon we had a crowd.

We heard this old man say, "Now that's talent. Raw talent."

Truman, he took his coonskin cap off, put it down on the floor, and said, "Y'all can contribute if you'd like." We was having a good time, got a huge crowd collected, but along come this policeman and another man who had a badge on said "Store Manager."

The policeman said, "Okay, where's the rest of your group?"

"What group?" I said. I was pretty scared because I didn't think we was doing nothing that would bring on the police.

"The rest of your group that's been stealing us blind," the store manager said.

"Stealing?" said Hertz. "We was just entertaining the folks." He waved his hand at the crowd. But as soon as he waved, everyone sort of scattered, disappearing into Paint & Wallpaper, or off into Electrical.

Truman folded his hands together like a little angel. "I'm a slow learner," he said. "I go to Reading Readiness."

"I think you all have some explaining to do," the policeman said. Then he got on his walkie-talkie and said something about "three suspicious individuals."

"But we was just here to collect boxes for our carnival," I said. Where would we explain? The police station?

"Ain't no carnival going on," said the store manager.

Truman picked up his coonskin cap and was kneading it like Play-Doh, and Hertz was standing with his arms folded, his army hat pulled down almost over his eyes. He looked like one of them criminals you see on TV trying to hide their identity.

And I was thinking, Oh Lord, this is the end of us.

Then out of Paint & Wallpaper come, who would have believed it, Superman swooping in for the rescue, good old Earl C.

He looked at me, he looked at Hertz and Truman. He looked at the officer and the manager. "What's going on here?" he said. He was holding a can of Rust-Oleum.

"Well, we don't know, exactly," said the manager. "We was just trying to find out."

"These is nice kids," Earl C. said.

"You know them?" the store manager asked.

"Yes, I do, and I'd be glad to take them home."

There was some discussion among the three of them. You could tell the store manager wanted to have us all hauled off, but the policeman said something about "no evidence."

Finally they all three sort of broke up and come walking toward us. "All right, I'll let you go this time," the store manager said, "but you'd better not let this happen again."

"No sir, it won't," I said in my best Junior Citizen voice, and we all three walked out with Earl C.

"Thanks, Earl C."

"Thanks, Earl C."

"Thanks, Earl C."

Hertz was the last one to pipe up. You could see he was sort of disappointed that we wasn't going to the police station. That would have made a better story to tell.

I'll say one thing. We was lucky it warn't Leroy that come into that hardware store. He'd have helped the police put us into the van and been proud to tell Mama she'd have to pick us up at the station.

Truman got his wagon and untied it. Earl C. put all them boxes into the back of his pickup, then put Truman's wagon on top.

"How about some chili?" he said. He was always real generous like that. One time last fall he'd took me, Hertz, Truman, and Annabelle to the Fiddler Creek Bluegrass Festival, paid our way, even bought us lunch.

Truman and Hertz sat in the back of the pickup and I sat up front with Earl C. We went down to Starcross Chili, all got into one big booth, and me and Earl C., we ordered us a Chili Two-Way. Hertz got two coneys, and Truman, he ordered a Chili Four-Way with extra cheese plus two coneys. I said, "Truman, Earl C. ain't made of money."

Earl C. said, "Whatever he wants, I just got paid."

In case you don't know what Chili Two-Way is, it's chili on spaghetti with lots of orange cheese on top. A Four-Way is the same, only with beans and onions. Truman, he loves them onions. Coneys is hot dogs with chili sauce on the top. We all ordered Cokes, except Earl C., he got coffee.

So we was all settling into our booth. Truman had a handful of straws he was blowing the wrappers off of, and Hertz, he'd already tried out the ketchup. Earl C. said, "What was you guys doing down there, anyway?" You could tell he was trying to be real casual.

Hertz sucked in his cheeks and looked at the ceiling, and Truman sort of stuck his tongue out one corner of his mouth, and me, I took a pack of sugar, opened it, poured a little out onto my place mat. Now was my chance. I'd get Earl C. to work on the carnival. Wouldn't even have to call him up.

So I said, "Oh, we was just practicing for a variety show."

"Variety show?" Earl C. said. "Tell me about it," and he put his arm around the back of the booth, real interested.

Now most any other grown person we'd have been with wouldn't have been taking us to no chili parlor after saving us from the police. He'd have been telling us how ashamed he was of being the center of such a scene. Thing is, Earl C. knowed that we wasn't never going to do nothing that stupid again, leastwise *I* wasn't.

So we started telling him about the carnival, about the booths and the variety show, and who was doing what, and right away he said, "I'll help out. What do you all need?"

That's Earl C. for you. I knowed he would want to help out.

"A truck. We need your truck."

Earl C. had one of them flatbeds, hauled hay on it in the fall. Me, Hertz, and Truman had been trying to figure out where we was going to do the talent show, but now I knowed. "We could use your flatbed like a stage." I could just picture us up there, doing our routines.

"You got it," he said. And then he said, "What's Annabelle up to? She doing anything for the carnival?"

"Quilts and crafts," I said. "She's raffling off a Birds in the Air quilt and running a booth with things the ladies at work are making."

"She always did make nice quilts." You could tell Earl C. didn't want to make no more comments. And I knowed that he knowed she was engaged to Leroy.

But I was going to bring them together. Earl C. must want to see Annabelle again, I thought, or he wouldn't be coming to the carnival or taking us out today.

I wouldn't tell Annabelle he was coming. Or Mama. If you told Mama, you might as well tell the world. And she would have had fits because she wouldn't want no competition for Leroy. I would just tell Mrs. Earlywine.

We had us a real nice time. And Earl C., he even told us a story. A good one, about a ring-tailed sidewinder that roamed the woods a-snatching bacon off the wagons of farmers and prospectors. That's one of them made-up critters like a snipe or a snarfus. But Earl C. can make them as real as a grizzly, doing all the sounds.

Mama wondered why I couldn't eat my supper that night, but I was still full from having chili with Earl C.

WEDDING SHOWER

Shirley Whirly come over to my house one Friday in April and seen my dress. "Ain't that beautiful," she said, touching the satin. "Real nice." But she couldn't stay long because she was going to her sister's wedding shower that night.

Wedding shower, I thought, what's that? Is that where everybody gets down and prays it don't rain on the wedding day? I didn't tell her I didn't know what it was, Shirley always thinking she was so smart and knowing more about weddings than I did. "That's nice," I said. "Have a good shower." Then as soon as Mama come home, I asked her, "What's a wedding shower?"

Mama said it was a party where everyone played a lot of games and brung presents for the bride, and that she was planning on giving Annabelle one as a surprise. "You'll be my helper," she said.

Wait'll Shirley hears about this, I said to myself.

Leroy had give Mama a list of the women at Rise'n'Shine who worked with Annabelle in the billing department. Me and Mama made out the invitations. They was all decorated with little flowers and umbrellas and said,

SURPRISE SHOWER FOR ANNABELLE

SATURDAY, MAY 4, A QUARTER TO 1:00 PM

621 CAPP STREET

P.S. PLEASE BE ON TIME.

WE WILL ALL BE HIDING IN THE KITCHEN WHEN LEROY

BRINGS ANNABELLE IN.

R.S.V.P. 555-3859

ASK FOR LAVERNIA KREBS.

The R.S.V.P. was Mama's work number. We didn't want nobody calling the house, since Annabelle might answer the phone. Mama, she kept telling me, "Don't you say a word to Annabelle. This is to be a secret."

And I kept saying, "Don't worry. I won't say a thing."

And I didn't.

Except to Shirley Whirly. On Monday, when she started a-bragging about her sister's shower, I just had to go and tell her about Annabelle's. "We're having petit fours," I said, hoping Shirley wouldn't know what a petit four was, "and raspberry punch, and playing a lot of games."

But Shirley didn't even ask. "I won two bottles of nail polish at my sister's shower," she said. "And ate a whole can of mixed nuts all by myself."

Shirley Whirly was pretty hard to top.

One day me and Mama got out our punch bowl—cut glass, Mama calls it—and all our little cups and we washed them up.

While we was working, I said to Mama, "You know, I don't think Annabelle really loves Leroy."

"Course she does," Mama said. "Why do you say that?"

"Well, she had more fun with Earl C. And Earl C. was nicer to her. She's just marrying Leroy because he's a big deal at Rise'n'Shine."

"Sometimes you have to put aside thoughts of love," she said, "and think about finances. Now your daddy's a smart man, and I love him, but he's content just to repair cars." Daddy worked down at Dillings Auto Shop, but he done a lot more than repair cars. He knowed all about what makes a car go, and he give lessons down there too, but the way Mama saw it, he was just a mechanic. "I think Annabelle's wise to go for management," she said.

The day of the shower, Daddy said he didn't want to be around for no hen party. He was going fishing. I was beginning to wish I could go with him. I didn't want to be playing no games with grown women.

The guests begun arriving around twelve-thirty. Mama had told them to park down on Prestige Avenue so Annabelle wouldn't see lots of cars in front of the house and suspect something. Dot Carver and Aurelia Kindness arrived first. They lived together in an apartment over on Commodore Parkway. They give Mama their presents, and she put them on the floor behind the buffet so Annabelle wouldn't see them when she come in. Then, Helen Walker, Sarah Beth Axton, and Thelma Dockum arrived. Alva Hubbard and Patsy Coe come after that. Sarah Beth and Patsy was to be Annabelle's bridesmaids.

The ladies was remarking on Miss Rise'n'Shine in front of the fireplace.

"He give it to Annabelle," said Mama.

"It's a beauty," said Dot Carver. "Though it's a shame he didn't win second prize. That was a dinner for two."

Annabelle and Leroy was supposed to be out hunting for curtains. Mama told everyone to get on into the kitchen and as soon as Annabelle come into the house, we would all yell, "Surprise!"

Well, we all waited at least ten minutes, everyone breathing heavy, giggling, whispering this and that, and then we heard a car door slam out front. The whole kitchen was clogged with perfume. Then we heard Annabelle's voice, sort of tired, and the door open, and her saying, "I don't care what color they are, just buy them!"

And I tell you, a thrill run through me. Annabelle was angry.

Mama shoved a chair across the floor and yelled,

"Surprise!" I knowed she was hoping to cover up the arguing going on. We all run in, Annabelle looking at us like we'd popped out of the woodwork. Old Leroy was just a-standing there smirking like his big-deal self, and saying, "You ladies have fun. I'm just a-going to take off."

Some of them ladies was calling him Mr. Cuzzens since he was their boss.

We all set down in the living room and then Mama said, in her best party voice, "Why don't we play some games? Mary Mae, you pass the pencils and paper." I done it, then Mama brought in her stopwatch and said we had three minutes to see who could figure out the most words in "Happy Shower." Everyone begun writing as fast as they could. Sarah Beth Axton was twisting her hair around her finger, Aurelia Kindness was tapping her eraser on the end table, and sometimes all you could hear was that little scratch of the pencils, *ts ts, ts ts*. I was looking for endings you could attach things to, like "ow" you could make into "how" and "sow" and "pow" and "row," but then Mama yelled, "Time!"

I had twenty-six words and I thought I done pretty good, but Aurelia Kindness had thirty, and Sarah Beth Axton had twenty-five, so Aurelia got the prize. Mama told me later that even if I'd got the most, I wouldn't have got no prize. That's because I was a hostess. I planned to tell Shirley Whirly I'd been a "hostess."

Then we played "Who, Blindfolded, Can Draw the Most Beautiful Bride?" Thelma Dockum done a good bride with a nice veil. I thought I done a pretty good job, but then I took my blindfold off and seen that the face I drawed was floating in outer space next to the head. Dot Carver, she was the only one that done a good face and a veil, plus she had little hearts on the skirt. We thought hers was the best.

Last game we played was "Honeymoon." I wanted to run out the door on this one, but Mama said I had to be Alva Hubbard's partner. I asked her why didn't *she* be Alva's partner, but Mama said she was working the stopwatch.

This is how you played: There was a suitcase with a nightgown and pajamas in it. You opened up the suitcase and one person was supposed to put on the gown, the other, the pajamas, and then you would race around into the kitchen and back into the living room. You would take off the night-gown and pajamas and put them back into the suitcase, and whichever couple done it the fastest—Mama was timing with her stopwatch—they would win.

Me and Alva went last, after Aurelia Kindness and Helen Walker.

Alva being so big, I didn't see how she would fit into the pajamas, I told her I would be the groom. Mama, she had her stopwatch, and she said "Go," so we was off. I got the pajamas on lickety-split, but Alva, she couldn't find the armholes to the nightgown, and once she found them, she put the whole thing on upside down. Well, just as we was tearing around into the kitchen, who should I see at the front window but Hertz and Truman. They had their noses pressed up on the glass and their hands cupped around their eyes, just eyeballing everything. Thought I would puke, them watching me.

Everybody was haw-hawing, including Hertz and Truman, who was making big nose prints on the window.

I went to the door and I said, real mean-like, "Mama wants you to scat."

Hertz said, real smug, "What's a-going on in there?" He had his music board with the cans.

And Truman, he said, "Is that a *shower*?" He was rubbing his cheeks with his sandpaper blocks.

I didn't answer, just slammed the door and watched them walk back over to Truman's.

Patsy Coe and Sarah Beth Axton won. They done it in twenty-three seconds.

I was hoping to sneak out as they was opening up their prizes, but Mama said I had to help her serve refreshments. She served the punch, and I handed out the petit fours.

Annabelle opened her presents while we was eating. She got place mats with pictures of the first eight presidents, a little crystal ice bucket, two sets of the silver pattern she'd picked out, a hand mixer, a tablecloth and matching napkins printed with red tulips, a kitty-cat wall clock, a mini-blender, a wooden salad bowl with a matching fork and spoon, and a set of iced-tea cozies.

"Of course you're coming back to work after your honeymoon," Thelma Dockum said.

"Oh, yes," said Annabelle.

"And where are you going to live?" Helen Walker asked.

"Leroy and I found ourselves an apartment in Mount Healthy," Annabelle said. "It's in an old house. We have us a private entrance on the side and four rooms on the second floor."

"Well, how nice," Alva Hubbard said.

"Right now, we're picking us out some curtains. Thing is, I want pink and he wants white."

"I say set your foot down," Dot Carver said. "A woman's got to choose her own curtains."

"Well, it's Leroy thinks I should listen to him."

Everyone could see they was getting into dangerous territory and wanted to avoid unpleasant talk at the shower, so they just moved on to reminiscing about their own weddings and showers. "Well, we was married on the Fourth of July," Thelma Dockum said, "and was it hot! I remember

Lucas, he lost his suitcase, so we had to go out and buy him all new clothes."

Patsy Coe said, "We was on a houseboat for our honeymoon. Went down to Memphis."

"Where are you going on your honeymoon?" Helen Walker asked.

"Leroy's thinking about the Poconos," Annabelle said. "He said he's found a place that's got an all-you-can-eat meal plan."

"Oh, well that's nice," Patsy said. "I seen the pictures in the magazines. Bubble baths in tubs shaped like champagne glasses. And heart-shaped beds. I think you and Leroy would like that."

Earl C. wouldn't be caught dead in a place like that, I thought to myself.

I'd had enough of that kind of talk, so I went and got a big poster of our carnival, asked them if they'd like to come. Most of them was already donating things to Annabelle's quilt booth.

Aurelia Kindness looked it over. "I think you should ask Mr. Cuzzens if he could donate some chickens."

"I already did."

"He said no?"

"Didn't have time for no kiddy carnival, he said."

Everyone kind of looked at each other as if to say, Well, that figures. I looked at Annabelle to make sure she was taking note.

But Mama come in with "It's probably not his place to be giving away chickens."

Then Patsy Coe begun talking about her cousin Caleb, how he got married to a nurse from Union City on a navy helicopter.

I got my guitar and snuck over to Truman's.

COUNTDOWN

Mrs. Earlywine was a-standing in the door with hairpins in her mouth, doing up a lady's hair, so she just sort of gestured that Truman and Hertz was out back somewhere. I went on through the house to the backyard.

They had turned over the old hair dryers Mrs. Earlywine kept out there and was riding them like horses.

"What was going on in there?" Hertz said. They was both smirking.

"I don't know," I said. "I was just helping out."

"Running around in them pajamas?" said Hertz.

"Warn't my fault," I said. I set my guitar down, kicked over one of the dryers and climbed onto the back of it.

Then we started trying to figure out what we

was going to do for the carnival. Hertz said we ought to sing "My Baby's Hot as Mustard," but I said no, we should do something new and special. I picked up my guitar and Hertz got his music board and Truman got his blocks, and they was swooping around the backyard, being bats and big-time singers, and sometimes clogging. (Clogging's something like tap dancing, only you stay in one place and just shuffle your feet.)

Then Truman, he'd go, "Little Lukey, Little Lukey" (and sort of do this clogging step and clap his sandpaper blocks), and Hertz, he'd do another clogging step and go, "Whatta kid, whatta kid, whatta kid, whatta kid" (and he'd be a-tapping and a-clanging his sound board), and me, I'd go, "If you want, if you want, if you want, if you want" (and I'd be a-strumming a tune on my guitar and then doing my own clogging step). And then we'd all come together and shuffle, like them stick-man dolls that dance on a board, and then I said, "Hey, let me write this down." Truman didn't have no paper handy, so I wrote it on a paper bag,

LITTLE LUKEY, LITTLE LUKEY, LITTLE LUKEY, LITTLE LUKEY

WHATTA KID, WHATTA KID, WHATTA KID, WHATTA KID

HE'S A TOW-HEAD, TOW-HEAD, TOW-HEAD, TOW-HEAD

HAPPY IN THE EAST

HAPPY IN THE WEST

HAPPY IS THE KID WE LOVE THE BEST

GIVE A WAVE, GIVE A HOOT

IT'S A KID WE SALUTE

LITTLE LUKEY, LITTLE LUKEY . . .

And we kept on a-going, making up more stuff and more steps, and raiding Truman's mama's closets for hats and vests, and we was just a-making up the best routine, and we done it and done it 'til we got it perfect. Truman even pulled off the cellar door and put it flat in the yard so we'd have a piece of wood to dance on.

Then we went over to Hertz's house, done it in the living room. It was nice in there, clogging on the wood floor, once we pushed everything out of the way. We was singing and dancing. Lordy, we was good.

Then we got out some Coca-Cola ice cubes

Hertz had made the night before, cooked up some pizza rolls in the microwave and dipped them into Cheez Whiz.

We knowed we was going to have something real professional for Little Lukey. We was making bigger and better plans since it was getting closer to the day. Down at the party store, we got us yards and yards of them crepe-paper streamers. We was going to put them all over, and the manager at Party Favors said the day of the carnival they'd bring by a hundred free helium balloons, all in spring colors, and paper cloths for our tables.

We even made a fancy chair for Little Lukey. We got a big old wooden bin, hammered a sunburst onto the back, and put a chair on top. It warn't that high, so Lukey and his mama and daddy could just step right up. We decided we'd put it in the middle of the street, right in front of Earl C.'s truck.

I called up Earl C. one night when Mama, Daddy, and Annabelle was out and told him he should park right in front of my house and get there by 9:30 a.m., before the police put up all the sawhorses at the end of the street.

Earl C. said he was going to have his truck decorated so it would look real nice. I wondered what Mama would say when he drove up.

Mama, she was a-running around making them popcorn balls, a-swearing under her breath something about a carnival and a wedding a week apart. You'd have thought she was the one a-getting married.

Leroy, he was a-coming around every night of the week now, saying to Mama what a wonderful thing it was what we was doing for Little Lukey, but not volunteering to do nothing hisself.

I said to Annabelle, "If I was getting married, I'd want whoever I was marrying to help out at the carnival."

"Mary Mae, I'm getting tired of you picking on Leroy," she said. This was the first time Annabelle ever got sharp with me. And it stung. But I sensed she was getting nervous about Leroy. And that was good.

Then Leroy come up from the cellar behind Mama with a jar of home-canned peaches. "Annabelle, you ought to learn how to can. On second thought, I don't even think you could. Maybe

I'm marrying the wrong woman." He chuckled. "Ought to be marrying Mrs. Krebs."

Annabelle's eyes welled up.

Not even Mama liked that remark. "Annabelle's a talented lady," Mama said.

But when I said to Mama, later on, "That wasn't nice what Leroy said, was it?" she stiffened up and said, "We all say things we're sorry for sometimes."

TROUBLE

Annabelle was a-putting the final touches on her quilt. She'd sewed all the squares together, and then she had to make what she called her "sandwich" of the quilt top—the stuffing inside, and the layer of muslin underneath. She brung all them things out on the lawn and pinned them together. Then, on a Thursday night, she took it to her church and the Senior Circle got together and quilted it. That means about eight of them, plus Annabelle, sat around a quilt frame—that's a couple of two-by-fours set on sawhorses—and made the tiny hand stitches through the sandwich. Annabelle had asked them if they wouldn't do this for Little Lukey.

I went with her, sat on a stool and drunk Coca-Colas from the church refrigerator. Mama was afraid I'd be bored with this and almost said I couldn't go, but Annabelle said, "No, I think Mary Mae will enjoy this." And I did. Besides that, I was proud to hear Annabelle stand up to Mama.

The satin glowed under them hanging fluorescent lights, and the ladies—most of them with white hair and glasses slipping down their noses—stitched up that quilt.

It was real peaceful in the room, the *pmp, pmp, pmp* of the needles going in and out, and a comment here and there.

"A quilt is something you can talk to," said one lady.

"If I couldn't quilt, I don't know what I'd do."

"It's something that you can be so proud of when you're done."

"And this one's a beauty."

"Birds in the Air."

"Makes me want to soar right up to heaven, just looking at it."

"How's the wedding plans a-coming?"

"Pretty good," said Annabelle.

"I hope he appreciates your talent. You got a real gift."

When they was finished, Annabelle brung her quilt home and put a border on it. Then she brung it into the dining room. Mama, Daddy, and I gathered around. "So much love," Mama said.

Annabelle was standing there feeling so proud, you could tell.

"Whoever wins this'll have a real treasure," said Daddy.

I couldn't wait 'til Earl C. could see it.

Leroy come over Sunday afternoon a week before the carnival. Annabelle had to run down to the store, so me, Mama, Daddy, and Leroy was a-setting in the living room, Leroy and Mama doing most of the talking. I had me my guitar on my lap, and I was just figuring out some chords, not talking or nothing, and Leroy, he'd been a-bragging to Mama about how he never shopped anywhere but the Celestial Star Grocery since they had the quality. Anyway, he out and said to me, "Mary Mae, if I was you, I'd get me a pie-ana."

"Pie-ana?" I said. "You mean a piano?"

Mama stiffened up in her chair. She didn't like me correcting an adult, especially Leroy.

"Whatever you call it," he said.

"Why?" I said. "This here guitar suits me perfect."

"Gee-tars ain't for ladies," said Leroy. "You know what gee-tars are for—"

I shook my head.

"They're for hillbillies."

Daddy sat up on that remark, though he didn't say nothing.

Mama said, "I offered to buy her a used pie-ana, but she likes her guitar." Mama seemed a little stunned by his remark, too. She played guitar a long time ago, but she give it up when she moved to the city. Said guitars reminded her of being poor.

Leroy put his lower lip up under his big front teeth and sucked. He done that sometimes when he was about to say something important. "How do you expect to rise in this world if you're going to play an instrument that's for hillbillies?"

"Hillbillies?" I said. "This guitar is my great-granny's. She was a musician and she made up her own songs. And she sung on the radio, too. *The Hidey Mountain Holler Show*." And then I stood up. I thought of walking out, but my feet wouldn't walk. And then my hands begun to strum, and my mouth begun to sing:

LEROY'S A PUMPKIN, LEROY'S A DREAD,

GOTTA GET LEROY OUTTA MY HEAD.

HE'S A BROWN SUIT, CLUCK-CLUCK,

MR. PRISS, RISE'N'SHINE,

UP-AND-COMER, WHEELER-DEALER,

CHICKEN PARTS A-GOING PLACES,

MR. CHICKEN, FINGER LICKIN'

CHEAP, CHEAP, STUFFED FUDGE

WALKIN' TALKIN' LEROY, TALK ABOUT YOUR LEROY

TALK ABOUT YOUR CHICKEN-PARTS CREEP!

Loud and clear I sung it, hitting all the chords perfect and making up the whole ending right there on the spot. I seen a smile start to come across Daddy's mouth, but he erased it real quick and just set tight. And I seen Mama's eyes get wider and wider, and her probably thinking she should stop me but setting there frozen in her seat. And Leroy swinging his head back and forth from Mama to Daddy like there was a big emergency, and he couldn't understand why nobody wasn't doing nothing.

But by the time I finished, he was setting there real smug like I'd proved what I was by singing that song.

So I knowed it had been the wrong thing to do.

"I'm sorry," I said.

Leroy didn't say nothing. Just looked off in the other direction.

Mama said, "I think Mary Mae and I need to have a few words."

Daddy walked out to the porch.

Mama and I went into the kitchen. "Mary Mae," she said. She took a big old serving spoon that was laying on the table and tapped out each word on her palm. "You will not sing at the carnival."

The house was so quiet I knowed Leroy could hear every word and I knowed he was just a-gloating over this.

"But the carnival's for Little Lukey."

"You can still do the carnival. But you are not singing."

"But I've got a song with Hertz and Truman."

"Hertz and Truman can sing it without you." Mama had put the spoon down, but she was still a-biting off each word.

"And I'm doing a solo."

"You'll not do a solo, neither."

Then I heard the front door. Annabelle was back, and her and Leroy was taking off to visit friends. I went up to my room. I stayed up there for a long time. I heard Mama leave. And then I heard Daddy outside in the garden.

He was turning dirt. He always done it in May, and had the seeds in by Memorial Day. I went downstairs, grabbed a shovel, and started helping him.

He didn't say nothing, so I started talking. "Daddy, I got to sing at the carnival," I said.

He kept on digging.

"I know I shouldn't have sung that song, but

you heard what he said about Great-Granny's guitar."

"Yes, I heard. And I got to admit, I couldn't blame you."

"Then why didn't you say nothing?"

"Mary Mae, you can't go around insulting people."

"No, I shouldn't have, and I learned my lesson. But I got to sing at the carnival. It's for Little Lukey."

Daddy shook his head. "That's how it goes."

I was tired of Daddy's not doing anything when Mama took over. And I thought, Well, things couldn't get much worse. So I yelled at Daddy. "Daddy, when are you going to stand up to Mama?"

"Don't you sass me, young lady."

"I'm not sassing you." And he knew it. He was just hiding. "Mama's a good person, but she's always doing things she shouldn't. Getting Annabelle to marry Leroy. And now she's trying to keep me from singing at the carnival. You know how important that is."

"You should have thought of that before you sung that song."

"I know I should have. I learned my lesson. But we're talking about something important. The carnival. Me, Hertz, and Truman, we put the whole thing together. Mama just don't see that. She don't see how important that is. It's not for me. It's for the Chassoldts."

Daddy turned another spade full of dirt. He didn't say nothing. Then he jammed the spade down in the dirt and scratched his arm. "I'll see what I can do," he said.

I put my shovel away and went back upstairs.

Things was real quiet in the house for the rest of the day. Leroy and Annabelle was gone. Hertz and Truman went to the show. I didn't want to go, because I was too upset. Probably wouldn't have been allowed to, anyway. I stayed upstairs.

I heard Mama come back, then sit down in the kitchen. Then I heard the back door shut. Daddy was inside. I crept over to the edge of the stairs.

"Lavernia, we got to talk."

"Yes, Farley, what about?"

He cleared his throat. "I think Mary Mae ought to be allowed to sing at the carnival."

"She's got a smart mouth and she's got to learn."

"Leroy said some things he shouldn't have," Daddy reminded her.

"Now don't go blaming Leroy," said Mama.

I expected Daddy to walk on down the hall. He never stuck around to argue. Ever. But this time he didn't back down. "I would say that Leroy was asking for it."

"What do you mean?" Mama asked.

"He shouldn't go insulting Mary Mae's talent and Great-Granny's guitar. Besides, your punishment is way out of proportion."

"She sung an ugly song. Now she don't get to sing."

Daddy cleared his throat. "You got to look beyond pettiness," Daddy said. "This is a big event Mary Mae has staged."

"Then she'll learn a good lesson."

But Daddy kept a-going. "What she'll learn is

to hate her mama, and I don't want her to do that."

Mama didn't say nothing. That almost never happened. I could hear her get up, open the refrigerator door, shut it, and walk across the kitchen. I liked to never thought she'd answer. "All right, she can sing. But she's got to be punished."

"She can turn the garden."

I crept back to my room.

When Annabelle come home, she walked right past me in the kitchen, didn't say nothing. So I knowed she'd only heard half the story. Even when I apologized next morning, she didn't say nothing.

CARNIVAL

Friday before the carnival, Shirley Whirly was a-going on at school about how "sweet" her sister's new husband was. How he brung her presents all the time and just made her so happy. They'd had their wedding the weekend before, already come back from their honeymoon to Chattanooga. "Where's Annabelle going for her honeymoon?" she asked.

I started to tell her, but I felt an ache in my throat grow into a rock and my eyes begin to burn, so I said, "Tell you the truth, I'm hoping she marries someone else." I felt real stupid. Shirley Whirly wouldn't understand.

"Marries someone else?" Shirley said. "But the wedding's next week."

Teachers at school made a big announcement about our carnival. The principal, Mr. Trimble, even announced it over the loudspeaker in the morning, and everybody was saying they was coming. Teachers was saying how proud they was of me, Hertz, and Truman.

But at home, Annabelle was barely speaking. At suppertime, she hardly looked at me. One thing I learned from Great-Granny, though, was even if things get rough, sometimes you got to carry on.

Everyone was getting their tables out the night before. Mrs. Earlywine had a truck from the Women's Business Association drop off panels for hanging things on, and extra tables for anyone who needed them.

At eight o'clock the morning of the carnival, the Party Favors store delivered the balloons, and me, Hertz, and Truman was tying them up everywhere.

Annabelle had set up all of her things outside at seven-thirty and gone back into the house for breakfast. Her Birds in the Air quilt was a real glory, hanging right behind her table on a line we'd strung between two poles.

Along about nine-thirty, just before the street was blocked off, Earl C. come down with his flatbed decked out in a blue-and-white gingham-checked skirt. He said he'd had it glued on by the Ladies Auxiliary of the DeSailles Volunteer Firefighters. Then over the top he'd built an arch out of wood and old baling wire, and he'd painted on the words "Capp Street Carnival." I showed him where to park it.

Leroy arrived about quarter to ten, all dressed up in a suit, probably didn't want nobody to think he warn't an executive. He rung the bell for Annabelle and then they both went out to Annabelle's quilt booth.

I seen her notice Earl C.'s truck. She was pointing at it and talking to Leroy.

I wasn't going to waste no time. I found Earl C. and brung him over to Annabelle's booth. "Earl C. brung his truck for the stage," I said to Annabelle and Leroy. "Ain't that nice?"

And then I walked off and watched from the porch. I wanted Earl C. to fall to his knees in front of the quilt. Or to yank it off the line, wrap it around Annabelle, and carry her down Capp Street through the crowd to Prestige Avenue. But they just started talking and laughing.

Nothing happened. Everybody was real friendly. Earl C. shook hands with Leroy. Annabelle talked and laughed. Leroy smiled. Earl C. smiled. Earl C. picked up one of the pot holders, flipped it back and forth like a pancake, put it back down, and then before you knew it, he was ambling off down the street.

I was feeling awful about this, but then I seen Little Lukey with his mama on their front porch and I knowed I had things to do. I had to find Hertz and Truman so we could drag Little Lukey's throne out beside Earl C.'s truck.

By ten, lots of people was walking up and down Capp Street. Shirley Whirly was there with her sister, Sallie Ann, who looked just like Shirley, and Shirley was wanting to know who Annabelle was. I pointed her out. And I pointed Leroy out, too. He was following the Channel Two News team, just a-hoping, I could tell, to be interviewed.

Shirley Whirly said to me, real confidential, "He's not that cute."

Me, Hertz, and Truman went and got the Chassoldts, and Little Lukey just set there on his throne like a prince on his mama's lap. He was laughing at all the balloons and people, and then the TV announcer come by, said, "Little Lukey, how about giving the folks out there a wave?"

I took Little Lukey from his mama, and me and Mr. Chassoldt showed him around all the booths, let him see what everyone was a-doing for him.

You never seen such a crowd as we got. People from church and Daddy's work, they was all there. And from school, lots of kids we knowed. And Mr. and Mrs. Chassoldt was saying hi to all kinds of people from the DeSailles Discount Outlet and the Hasenour Bottling Works.

Hertz's daddy's band played at eleven, not so loud as they usually played, Hertz said. That was so everybody could talk.

Annabelle was a-running her quilt booth and dropping them raffle tickets into a big pickle jar. Tickets was ten dollars a piece. Dot Carver was helping her sell.

Well, I knowed I should have been happy, what with all the money we was making for Little Lukey, but Earl C. hadn't run off with Annabelle, and

Leroy was strutting around, chest out like a big turkey.

Then a miracle happened. I was standing near Annabelle's quilt booth when the reporter come up to her. "This is a mighty fine piece," he said, putting his hand behind the quilt and holding it out to the camera. Annabelle looked so pretty and full of confidence, I knowed that's why he came up to her. "Where did you learn how to quilt?"

"My mama taught me before she died. And my grandma and great-grandma, they all done quilts, too. It's a Birds in the Air quilt," she said, touching one of the blocks.

Leroy seen the reporter talking to Annabelle, so he come up hisself. Didn't want Annabelle to get all the attention. Then the reporter put the question to Leroy. "What do you think of this lady's work?"

Well, Leroy, he stood there for a second like *he* was the prize. You could tell by the way Leroy puffed hisself up he was about to say something smart-aleck. And if he did, I just knowed it would set Annabelle off. Them quilts meant more to her than anything in this world. Finally Leroy cleared his throat, wet his lips, brushed a fleck of popcorn off his suit. "I think these quilts is nice, but I think she ought to join the twenty-first century and buy herself a bedspread that's all of one piece."

Leroy expected everyone to chuckle, or at least to agree with him, but nobody did.

Annabelle turned white.

The reporter backed off and went on down to Percy and Sue Macon's cornhusk dolls. I seen Earl C. take a deep breath and look as if he couldn't believe what Leroy had said. Even Mama looked shocked.

Leroy started to talk to Annabelle, but she stared straight ahead. More than that, I never seen Annabelle get so mad. She slammed her calculator down, walked out of that booth, and stormed into the house.

Leroy looked real puzzled, like one of them Rise'n'Shine chickens coming off the truck. He said to Mama, "Mind if I follow her in?"

Mama said, "I don't mind, but I think Annabelle needs to be alone." Mama was right about that. Leroy set out on the front porch for I don't know how long.

A thrill run through me. Things was going right at last.

At noon we gathered everybody around the stage for the variety show. Cleon Riddle done all the announcing. Being a clown, he was good at it. He told a few jokes first. "Did you know I proposed to my wife in the garage?" he said. "That way she couldn't back out."

Ernest Childers done his trained-parrot act first, and then Verlie Wickoff twirled fire batons. Little Lukey, he liked that. He was setting on his mama's lap just a-kicking and a-pointing away. Janice and Loretta Nonesuch come next. They climbed onto the back of Earl C.'s truck, and Cleon said, "Now I want to introduce, straight from DeSailles, by way of Baghdad, Janice and Loretta, the Nonesuch sisters, who will perform a belly dance to the tune of 'The Sheik of Araby.' " And each of them gals had these little bells they was ringing.

Then me, Hertz, and Truman done our tribute to Little Lukey. Hertz's daddy's band played a little background rhythm, and I tell you it was something. People was applauding and applauding, especially the Chassoldts.

Cleon introduced me next. "Now we have a talented little lady with her own special song, Miss Mary Mae Krebs."

I come back up. Everybody was a-smiling, so I was feeling real good. "This here gospel song I'm a-going to sing was wrote by my great-granny. I found it in her box of songs, only it didn't have no chorus. Great-Granny didn't finish that part, so I finished it for her." Mama and Daddy was a-looking up at me. I could tell they thought I was doing a real good job. "It's called 'Put Your Troubles in the Gutter, God's A-Sweeping Streets Today.' " I strummed a few chords, then lit in:

PUT YOUR TROUBLES IN THE GUTTER,

GOD'S A-SWEEPING STREETS TODAY.

HE WILL SPIN HIS WHIRLING BRISTLES,

HE WILL WIPE YOUR CARES AWAY.

HE WILL DROP THEM IN THE HOPPER,
HE WILL SWEEP UP ALL YOUR SHAME,
GOD'S DESCENDING WITH HIS DUMPSTER,
LET US PRAISE HIS HOLY NAME.

SING HALLELUJAH, GOD'S A-SWEEPING,
GOD'S A-SWEEPING, YES IT'S TRUE.
GOD'S A-SWEEPING UP YOUR TROUBLES.
YES, HE CARES FOR ME AND YOU.

IF YOU'VE GOT A LIFE OF RUBBISH
AND YOU DON'T KNOW WHAT TO DO,
BRING IT OUT AND PUT IT CURBSIDE,
HE WILL SWEEP IT UP FOR YOU.
AND IF YOU'RE THINKING THAT YOUR BURDENS
ARE TOO MUCH FOR YOU TO BEAR,
JUST REMEMBER GOD HAS BRISTLES,
HE WILL SWEEP UP ALL YOUR CARES.

SING HALLELUJAH, GOD'S A-SWEEPING,
GOD'S A-SWEEPING, YES IT'S TRUE.
GOD'S A-SWEEPING UP YOUR TROUBLES.
YES, HE CARES FOR ME AND YOU.

I tell you, I got everybody a-clapping and a-hollering. Mama, she was standing in the front row clapping like I never seen her clap before. Channel Two News was a-taping away. And then everybody was joining in on the chorus. I felt like I was twenty feet high.

I just finished and this man come over and said, "You wrote that yourself, little lady?"

"Yes," I said. "What my great-granny didn't finish."

"Well, I'd like to have you sing for *The Merry-Makers Talent Review* on Channel Thirty-two." He give me his card, asked for my number, and said he'd call up Mama and Daddy. I was so excited, I couldn't believe it. I watched that show all the time. They had singers and dancers and acrobats, and I always did think I could do as good as those kids on TV.

Then a reporter said to Cleon, "All right, who's in charge of this carnival?"

"These kids right here," Cleon told him, and pointed to me, Hertz, and Truman, so the man with the microphone had us climb back up on the truck.

"What inspired you to do this for Little Lukey?"

"Well, we knowed he had a bad heart," I said, "and we wanted to make him some money."

"What a wonderful idea. And you organized this yourselves?"

"Yeah, my mom helped," Truman said.

"And all the neighbors pitched in," I said.

"And the folks down at Party Favors give us free balloons and streamers," Hertz said.

The announcer said something about having hope for the leaders of tomorrow with kids like us, and give us each a handshake.

I was feeling so happy I thought I'd burst.

MELODY INN

Annabelle never did come back out of the house. Dot Carver run Annabelle's booth alone for the rest of the day, and some woman from Erlanger won the quilt. Then about two o'clock I seen Leroy leave. He was a-walking through the crowd holding Miss Rise'n'Shine over his head like a drumstick.

I got goose bumps just watching him leave.

We sold out of everything by four.

Earl C. helped Mavis Truffle pack up her parachute, then put it on the back of his truck. I was disappointed to see them drive off together, but I couldn't wait to find out what happened between Annabelle and Leroy.

She never even come out of her room for the rest of the day. I didn't knock. Whatever had happened with her and Leroy, I knowed she needed to be alone.

Finally, Sunday morning, Annabelle come down-stairs. Real cheerful. Fixing herself some cereal, she begun leaking out to me that she realized Leroy warn't the man for her, up-and-comer though he was. She said she told Leroy he would just have to find someone else.

"Yes?" I said, hoping she would give me more details, and she did.

He had said to her, "It ain't possible to break up now because we got a deposit on our refrigera-tor."

So Annabelle had said to him, "You can just get a refund."

He'd told her, "You got a hope chest full of presents."

Annabelle said, "I can give them all back, in-cluding the hope chest."

He told her, "Don't forget we both work at Rise'n'Shine."

She told him, "I, for one, can get a job any-where else."

He told her, "I'll just have to take Miss Rise'n'Shine."

"So I handed her to him," said Annabelle. "I

had to force myself to be polite and not pitch that chicken out the door."

It was a thrill to hear Annabelle, fierce as a cat.

Fact is, Annabelle went to work Monday and offered to give back all her presents, but the ladies insisted she keep them for when she found the right man. Except for Alva Hubbard. She wanted her iced-tea cozies, she said, for her sister Ruth.

"You was right all along, Mary Mae," Annabelle said. "I should have listened to you."

I tell you, I was in rapture. Annabelle was broke up with Leroy and the carnival was a huge success. We made $3,432.69, which me and Daddy counted on Saturday night and took to the bank Monday afternoon. Six hundred dollars of that was from Annabelle's quilt booth. Once it was deposited in Daddy's account, he wrote a check and me, Hertz, and Truman went over to present it to the Chassoldts. On top of that, there was two anonymous donors seen us on TV and they donated another one thousand dollars each.

The Chassoldts was just a-hugging us, saying, "Thank you, thank you."

With that money and all that was collected in the tins all over town, plus other donations that come in, Lukey had enough for his heart operation.

I thought Shirley Whirly would be a-rubbing it in to me when she heard there wasn't going to be no wedding, but she said to me, real serious, like she was a wise old woman, "You got to be sure it's the right one." Then she said, "I seen that Leroy on the TV news Saturday night, what he said. He's a real turkey."

I was just happy that Annabelle finally set up and took notice. That carnival made her see that she's worth something. That she can do things. That she didn't have to put up with a Leroy.

Annabelle even had the nerve to give two weeks' notice, go find another job at Mellwood Electric, and sign up for a summer night-school class in accounting.

"What's she going to do with the dress?" Truman wanted to know.

"She can save it for when she marries someone else," I said.

Earl C. went out with Mavis Truffle, the sky-diver, for a while after the carnival. We seen his truck down the street a few times. And Annabelle went out once or twice with Hertz's daddy, Seymour. You could tell Mama didn't like that, thought Hertz's daddy was too wild for Annabelle, with his fringed jacket and his ponytail, but she knowed she'd better bite her tongue.

Then one day Earl C. stopped by. Annabelle knowed he was coming, just hadn't told us. Me and him had a nice chat in the living room. Mama come out to say hi. Two weeks later, Earl C. and Annabelle was engaged.

Was I ever riding high, not to mention how joyous Annabelle was. Earl C. brung her all kinds of presents, an old-time basket she could use to put quilt scraps in, some Coca-Cola bottles filled with wildflowers, and a butterfly carved out of wood.

Had their wedding in December and I tell you, it was a wedding to behold. Bridesmaids, we wore them mint green dresses Annabelle and me had picked out, and they looked just perfect with the holly and the poinsettias. For their honeymoon, they went to Cumberland Falls, where it turns out Annabelle had been wanting to go all along. They had a big wedding dinner at the Melody Inn with carolers that come in from DuRoss. I tell you, that Earl C., he done things right. The whole wedding party, we all come over in about six or eight vehicles.

You never seen Annabelle so happy.

Even Mama, she said, "You know, I think Annabelle has made herself a fine choice."

What they was going to do was live in Earl C.'s apartment until spring and then they was going to move down to Earl C.'s cabin. Earl C. would start his repair shop and plant a little corn, and Annabelle would quilt and do Earl C.'s accounting books. In fact, Earl C. expected her to make a little money on her quilts.

ELVA

With Annabelle moved out, Mama put an ad in the paper.

ROOM FOR SINGLE WOMAN

NON-SMOKING, CLEAN LIVING

—EVENING MEALS

—KITCHEN PRIVILEGES

—REASONABLE RENT

I asked Mama what did "kitchen privileges" mean. It didn't seem to me that being in the kitchen was any privilege, but she said that meant the person could come in and make herself a sandwich anytime she pleased.

A woman named Margaret looked at the room, said she was hoping for an area where there would be more single men.

"Oh, but our last girl didn't have no trouble," Mama said.

Margaret said she would keep the room in mind.

Then there was this woman named Iona, asked Mama if she minded if she did the cooking in the evening. Mama said, "I wouldn't *mind* so much having a break now and then, but it seems as if I might have to reduce your rent if you do it."

"Yes, that's what I had in mind," Iona said.

"I'm afraid we need all the rental money we're asking. Maybe you'll have better luck elsewhere."

Soon's Iona left, Mama said to Daddy, "Imagine the nerve of that woman, suggesting she be allowed to cook so that her rent can be lowered."

"Can't blame her for trying," Daddy said.

And then a woman named Elva took the room. She don't have no boyfriends, but she's real nice and runs the Merle Norman makeup store out at the mall.

Little Lukey, he had his operation and he's going to preschool next year.

Annabelle and Earl C. just moved down to Earl C.'s cabin. She's got a sign hung out on the porch,

QUILTS! QUILTS! QUILTS!

They're adding a room on the back, and Annabelle's making a Tumbling Blocks quilt.

Me, Hertz, and Truman ain't doing stunts anymore. Truman stays after school for Enrichment, and Hertz's house finally got torn down for that apartment, so he lives two blocks over. But he visits sometimes, brings me presents—a harmonica he found at the bus stop, some more guitar picks, a calendar of the mountains. He even pointed out a cabin in one of the pictures and said, "Me and you should live here someday." Imagine that!

Right now I'm practicing for the *Hometown Hayride* show. They signed me on for five appearances after they seen me on *The MerryMakers Talent Review.*

Shirley Whirly got her whole family around the

set for *MerryMakers*. "Now that girl's a terror of a talent," her daddy said.

And Mama, when she was walking me out of the studio, paid me the nicest compliment. "Just like Great-Granny used to play."

Acknowledgments

I would like to thank my editor, Janine O'Malley, for her guidance in bringing Mary Mae front and center, and especially for her patience and good humor.

I would like to thank my agent, Ann Farber, and her husband, Don, for their counsel and friendship.

Thank you to my copy editor, Janet Renard, a former Kentuckian, who knew what I meant when I called a house "shotgun."

Thanks also to Lore Segal, for her enthusiasm for the manuscript in an early form.

Thank you to James Papa and Laurie Siegel, who also offered sound advice.

And to Susie Wood Smith, who described for me what it was like to be a child singer.

Thank you to the members of the Bloomington and Louisville writers' groups who generously offered their critical remarks: Elaine Alphin, Marilyn Anderson, Judy Carney, Joy Chaitin, Michael Ginsberg, Keiko Kasza, Marcia Kruchten, Bobbie Larkin, Elsa Marston, Pat McAlister, Pamela Service, Lynn Slaughter, and Amanda Stanley.

Finally, to J. P. Fraley, founder of the J. P. Fraley Mountain Music Gatherin' in Carter Caves State Park, Kentucky: I attended because I wanted to hear mountain music at its best. You did not disappoint. Thank you for a spirited lineup that captured the essence of Kentucky.